I0730230

Carrion Bloom Books
carrionbloombooks.com

Jace Brittain and Rachel Zavecz, Editors

I Wander the Earth, Hungry for Semen
© 2025 Cat Ingrid Leeches

ISBN 978-1-7347662-7-1

Cover Art: Jace Brittain
Interior Images: WL
Book Design: Rachel Zavecz

I wander the earth, hungry for semen

Cat Ingrid Leeches

carrion BLOOM BOOKS

drawings by
WL

Confessionals, Seances, Manifestos, Fragments, Dream
es, Myths, Fairytales, Incubations, Episodes, Stor
Contents, Fables, Chapters:

Freezer

Dog

I dream that I take a man home with me from the bar.
His penis is a single strand of floss that unspools across the floor (perhaps I am being generous in this description) (We all know that it hung limply b/t his legs, not even hitting the back of his knees), I weave it between my teeth, grateful that I could make love without taking off my clothes.

You should know: when I turned thirteen I grew a marsupial pouch.

When the surgeon removed my appendix and took my shirt off, he was embarrassed for me.

How can you be so obscene?

I thought you were my surgeon and not my lover. Why would you care?

What could you possibly store in there?

He filled it with soil and stapled it shut. He fancied that he had a green thumb.

If you put your hand there—no, there, press down, but not too hard—you can feel earthworms writhing underneath the skin.

Or maybe that's just a tapeworm.

When my mother was drunk, she wanted to turn me,
fill me with the amphibious. Only frog eggs for breakfast (or were they eyes?)

There is a dead dog in my freezer, I tried to tell the surgeon.

Yes, yes, I know. He thinks I'm referring to my sister. (All the men are in agreement—she was a real animal).

A pouch must be cleaned and picked. And now that mine is stapled shut, it smells just as much as the next body.

*

Fertilizing bats is my job.

They destroy entire agricultural systems in countries far away from mine.

Why can't I care.

I don't even dream about it.

My father was a bomb maker (my mother called him the unmaker, hissed it b/t her gap tooth). I used to think that was the same as a florist. She felt the need to count his fingers and toes, check meticulously for breaks in the skins, before he was allowed to sit at the table.

With those fingers, he taught me to lace up my shoes. I always forgot how, until my hands were in his. (Did he move my fingers for me?)

He's long dead, but there's a moment when I look down at my shoes—are his fingers still, somehow, moving my body? Is the dead man reaching through the soles of my feet, wearing my hands like gloves?

I am nothing like my father.

His hands touched bombs that turned people into a nutritious pink mist for the insects and rats, the only species who could survive his kind of violence. My hands touch strange children, combing viscous (vicious) pollen and spells through their fur, transferring love from my body into theirs.

You see, these are entirely different matters.

My children seem to thrive off sulfuric air.

They were made for this new world.

We have learned to inhabit concepts as skins. You need many skins to even go outside anymore. My favorite skin is composed of the difference between what I say and what I mean.

I used to hate it; now it is me.

My second favorite skin is the pride in my winged children.

Our country thanks you for your service.

Have you, Have you, been a murdered/child?

Have you, Have you, seen them?

Freezer dog is an emblem of my childhood.

My mother stored dead cats in an industrialized tundra: layers of ice, fur, and plastic that looked geological. Their eyes like fish eyes.

My eyes.

In there, she also kept the garlic bread served exclusively to my father—a secret. At night, the cats would swirl together and bang against the lid.

Until I let them out.

I have never told this to anyone. I have lived with guilt for a long time, and maybe that's why my children fly across the world with murderous intentions.

The cats, in their anger, perforated my mother's womb.

That's how my imaginary sister was born.

A girl made of shadow, except I knew what she really was: cats in a sack of primordial skin, twisted with fury. I could see their glowing teeth inside her, like the veins in my own wrists. When my mother was in the room my sister was   oh so silent,   but I still talked.

When she was gone, my sister would swipe her claws against my cheek.

I know you have teeth, why don't you use them, she said.

A ghost that never gives it up disappears without ever knowing, I read.

I tried desperately to teach her that she wasn't real, so she could make herself real. But she wouldn't believe me.

We were born of the same womb, she said.

But I doubt myself.

And one day she was gone, but not before my cheeks were shredded. I wish I could have shown her my pouch. Pressed her hand into its warmth. I think the men were right—she was a real animal—and would have known what to do when

*

I woke up on my fifteenth birthday with as many legs as a crab, my skin chitinous. My mother treated me like nothing strange had happened and still made me go to school that day.

Don't be a baby, she said. But I ache.

Unlike my mother, my classmates noticed.

And I could see in their eyes, a question:

How did the processes of your body escape us? Why are you undergoing further transmogrifications?

I want to suck your juices dry, a boy whispered.

And I knew his words for what they were: a threat against my existence.

But I didn't mind anymore. When I got home, my mother boiled me.

The legs fell off. The marsupial pouch was dry, with flakes of skin and other such detritus.

I had to massage my insides for two years with oregano oil before I let anyone else in.

And oh,,,,,,,,,, how it burned.

● ●

Premonitions of a Valley Girl
(to be read in upspeak)

My daughter is missing a uvula.

Her cat speaks for her when she places her fingers lightly on the nape of neck
with a somewhat threatening flourish. His mouth opens on cue:

it sounds like the groaning of an ancient house
I open the ground with a shovel
trying to dig up what I imagined
the last tenants left behind, buried,
too heavy to take with them.
With a simple heave, the shovel's tip already embedding in the flesh,
the whole top comes loose?

As if the topsoil was dead skin on my foot that I could peel back and reveal
what was
underneath,
but it's still dead down there, not new and baby pink like I thought?

It goes thousands of miles deep but   all   still   dead

I don't have a daughter?

Many of my friends have daughters? Their lives crisscrossing in different directions than mine.

Some of them even have dead daughters?

My mother and me would take trips to the cemetery, bring a picnic basket or, more often, a six-pack of Sprite.

An excuse for ritual.

Here are the prohibitions of our ritual:

DO NOT STEP where a dead body could potentially be. For safe measure assume dead bodies occupy a space that is at least three-and-a-half feet wide and seven feet in length starting at the tomb stone. (Back then I thought only tall men had the right to be buried, but I have never unthought this thought?)

DO NOT THINK dirty thoughts while looking at the headstone, or even at the ground, or even while thinking of the dead and what their life must have been like, and wondering if their wife is still alive (and if she got remarried to their twin brother and how often do such things happen?) It invites the dead into your dirty kind of dreaming.

Breathe softly. Do not breathe badly: yawning, sighing, groaning, and whining are all offenses in this category. (My voice is a physical protuberance, a large elongated mole that starts at the back of my throat and grows all the way out of my mouth?)

IT IS OKAY to make fun of garish headstones (i.e. big breasted angels weeping over the dead) these individuals probably aren't popular with the dead anyway. Even the dead have a social hierarchy that must be respected—

(rotting does not equal anarchy?)

What does it mean to be without a uvula? (Sometimes I think I have a daughter
who is missing a vulva?)

What does it mean to talk through a cat?
Who opens his mouth
and everyone is instantly transported to an old and scary house?
The kind that in your childhood, made your piss your pants
a little any time you looked at it.

I didn't know girls had to change their jeans more often than men? An older
boy told me, you smell like cunt. I thought this meant I was fuckable and my
skin glowed for days and days?

Does this mean my daughter is a haunted house?
Does this mean my daughter
dreams of occupying a haunted house? Dreams in houses?
Dreams in age?

In either case, it is unnatural. No one would disagree with this sentiment.

I promise to bite off her hands after she is born. Baby hands look like
bubblegum, soft and pre-digested. Maybe if she has no hands you will refrain
from killing her and me?

If dead children return, really I am alone. None of my friends will come out
to play.

After my daughter died I was alone,

and my house was so silent?

It took me WEEKS to learn the sounds of this silence?
In the early morning hours
I first heard the house talking to me. Here is its vocabulary:
murmurations and groans. There are many types of groans.
My favorite was the way the house
shifted its weight from foot to foot.
I did not know I was living inside a living?

And even though my daughter was dead, the cat refused to leave. I bolted the
front door, and he moved through the walls like they were nothing.
One night, I opened his jaws and looked inside, searching for the cat's uvula.
His breath was a sour ocean, the top of his soft palate rotting. He should go to
a doctor, I thought? He will die soon, I thought?

Inside his mouth there was so much I had not known about my daughter, so
much I had not known about myself?

My head fell into his, and his body into my body?
Will I be better in a different life?
Will I be good and kind?

In another world I am sure, I am so sure of this, we all decided to remove our
eyes? Spread them on toast, or whatever food item you prefer, and eat them.
And then for the rest of our lives we told each other stories about these eyes?

YOU WON'T BELIEVE ME but mine were fantastic. Blue around the rim.
Mine were so dark, they looked like mud. And we talked and talked about
those eyes and nothing else. Mine were just okay, but in that world I believed
they were the jewels of angels?

I've never seen dark, or rather, I've never seen nothing?
When I turn out the lights my eyes play tricks on me.

Like me, I do not think they like the idea of being alone, of not existing.
                    Maybe this is how my daughter-not-daughter was born.

I lift the folds of my lover's stomach,
OH MY GOODNESS,
oh my goodness

I have never rated my lovers on a scale of 1 to 10, never articulated the level
of attractiveness of my lovers?

I have only been in awe of their form. It is too many details to take in, to come
up with some sort of conclusion?
But I am capable of revulsion. But maybe maybe maybe maybe that is only in
rememory after you have left me?
I see warnings, maybe?
Or are those premonitions on your body that you will hurt me?

Do you think if I had looked closer, somewhere on your body would be
a warning:
my sperm will give you a daughter
missing a uvula,
who is really a haunted house.
Do you think there would be another warning?

You are gestating inside your own child, an inversion of telescoping
generation—practically human aphids?
And you will take her cat for a lover not sure if he was really the father,

or if you just fell into his mouth?
And if that was just an act of devotion,
or he really intended to eat you—daughter, old house, and all?

You have a sensation of falling

and at night you have trouble telling where your skin is, where your fingers
are? Where your feet and the earth differ? But you peeled it back, ruined it
for all of us. And we are standing thousands of feet beneath where we used
to stand?

• •

Melt

The young girls my father murdered are buried in my mother's garden.

There are worse fates.

My mother is a horticulturist and creates a new variety of apple tree in honor of each dead girl, except she refuses to call them apples (or dead girls) and says those words are bastardizations of the glorious history of the fruit and its complicated relationship to the brutality of mankind. She calls them "melt-in-the-mouths" and "tongue-roses." She tells me each dead girl has a mother somewhere mourning her, just like these trees sometimes harbor resentment toward their fruit. My mother extracts locks of hair from the bodies, carefully preserving the integrity of the strand, and grafts them to the bark. She scrapes skin cells from the bottom of their dead girl feet and feeds these to the roots. I am disturbed. Before the girls are covered by dirt, I stare at their faces. They are barely older than me.

I have never seen my father. I hear his footsteps in the house. In the morning I smell echoes of his aftershave & mouthwash. Otherwise his smell is entirely his own, meaning I cannot dissect & separate its components. When he uses the toilet, showers, or spits, he leaves behind a scent that is distinctive from my mother and me and therefore threatening. Even when he washes well, and he is not a man who values cleanliness, the scent remains pungent and drowns out my own scent, which might as well be nonexistent. Because as far as the neighbors know my father has neither a wife nor daughter. We have not seen my father. The neighbors have not seen us. We have seen the neighbors. But only when we are bad, pull back the curtains, and spy on them using a handheld lens.

This is not allowed. The neighbors are very tall. The neighbors have very clean hands with long fingers, and at the end of each finger is a bird. Sometimes the birds come alive, but the neighbors are quick to snap their necks and the birds are dead again and the hands belong to them & are useful once more. I imagine they would be immensely embarrassed if this occurred outside the sacred intimacy of the home. What happens when the birds come alive if they are at work or on a date? I do not know. I like to think that the bird gets to take their place, and the humans are severely punished. I imagine the bird is let loose into the world and it will eclipse all sources of light and warmth (for the guilty party) and the human in question will never know joy again.

Our neighbors all carry little knives with them. And by little, I mean these knives are bigger than the length of my arms but smaller than the knives I see in my father's kitchen that he might use on the girls if they refuse to go quietly, but they always go quietly. I have never seen any gashes on the girls' bodies. They graciously agree to die. And I think, if my father ever asks me to die for him, even though he is my father, I will scream, and the neighbors will become aware of my existence, and all the birds at the end of their fingers will come alive at once. And they will eat the apples in the tree. And they will be

filled with the voices of the dead girls. And the voices of the dead girls will
return to their mothers and they will tell their mothers what my father has
done to them and the mothers will destroy us all.

One day this happens. I scream. My father isn't around, I guess I scream
because I am lonely or because the possibility of screaming has always been
there. And yes, the birds come alive. They eat the apples from the tree. A week
later the mothers are here, in the house, hunting my father. They ignore me
entirely. I make myself small in a corner. I piss myself. I can't stop sniffing my
clothes, and I am enchanted—for once my scent is the loud one. When I see
the mothers clutching their even bigger knives and bragging to one another
about how blood thirsty they are, I think this is the end. I could care less. One
by one the mothers disappear, I hear them moaning through the walls. They
are being murdered. Later, my mother tells me, just like their daughters, they
have succumbed to my father. Their bodies are buried in shallow graves on
top of their daughters or next to their daughters, although the daughters are
badly decomposed and it is hard to match up kin. But we do not create new
varieties of apple trees for the mothers because we are angry with them. And
the trees seem angry too. The fruit on the branches spontaneously rots and it
smells so bad that it is impossible to perceive that the mothers, buried mere
inches beneath the surface, are rotting too.

:::::::::::::::::::::::::::::::::

A Lover is a house

What is this*, **my lover asked, peering between my legs,**
There's a string. I immediately assumed I had forgotten a tampon inside of
me, even though it had been more than a week since I bled. I imagined a
cotton thumb swirling with crustaceans and psychopathic bacteria, ready
to kill me at the first sign of weakness in my body's defenses. My mother
warned me such things could happen. When you are older you become
forgetful, she said. And I understood forgetfulness was a euphemism, but I
wasn't old enough to understand it and I'm still not.

Except she wasn't my mother, she was a *mother*—

A video cassette my father brought home one night to help me sleep. The
woman's face, a generic composite of all the motherly faces in the world. But
maybe that's why I don't understand her wisdom—it's just always a little bit
off, meant for one of her other daughters, or designed to serve all of us, so
really none of us. And I wondered what she would do with a daughter like
me anyway, one who—

Before I could reply to my lover, he tugged on the string. It was tangled up
in hair: p i n   p r i c k s: a n   o p e n i n g: d   e   f   o   r
e   s   t   a   t   i   o   n —

When I opened my eyes, his fist had been transformed into a giant squirming
slug.

And that's when I knew someone had done a bad sort of magic on us,
and our love was doomed.

wasps burrow into my body
while I sleep, the same way men do. I have never hated a species
as much as I hate our own.

His transformation continued throughout the night—
my lover became a snail; my house his shell.

My father was pissed. *Make him take it off.*
I ignored him and dipped my hand into my lover's flesh.
He's oozing all over the neighborhood. In fact, you both are.

What I didn't finish telling you before is that I am skinless. Intestines wrap
around my throat and shine like rubies in a certain light. I sprinkle drying
powder on my organs so that my entire body doesn't *glisten* obscenely.

My boyfriend becoming a snail did not weaken the sexual aspects of our
relationship like you might assume. In fact, I enjoyed sharing a bed with
something as soft and vulnerable as myself. Sometimes, he would dilate one
of his pores so I could breathe effortlessly while my body floated inside his.
And I would close my eyes and pretend to be weightless in space.

This made our doomed love all the more horrible in the end.

I showed my father a map of snail anatomy. Showed him where the heart was in our home, the stomach, even the gonads (which were located in the attic) (which was maybe why so many birds had taken to pecking the shingles off of our roof).

My father was not heartless enough to kill my lover, but he could not get over having to witness our love-making at all hours.

I cannot tell whose slime is whose, and in some states, this would be criminal.

He set up a tent in an empty lot three streets down.

I had a dream that I was an animal—splayed hips, hooves, and fur. The land was covered in eucalyptus trees that barely brushed my ribcage. Someone gutted me like a fish and fucked me in my wound, yet I still tried to walk forward. In my dream, my sheer enormity meant that I was not used to being helpless.

When I wake up inside my lover, I can feel infestations all around us, birds, snakes, bats, rats, and insects. All trying to get inside our home.

We both know infiltration and death is inevitable.

I watch his beating heart while I make a fungi omelet in the kitchen. I am careful to keep the spice cupboard closed. I couldn't imagine living without rosemary, coriander, even the simplicity of thyme. But my lover flinches away at the memories of certain foods now. His thoughts translated into sensations.

I hear a rap-tap-tap-tap on the kitchen window, and when I peek behind the curtains, thousands of eyes meet mine. Their gaze shifts beyond me and they gorge themselves on the sight of his heart.

I can't help but wonder, should I take the first bite?

It's my father's voice inside my head, but no, no, no—genetics is no excuse—I thought that thought into existence.

Have I told you about my birth?

There were two women who gave birth, their rooms on opposite ends of a hospital corridor, but somehow there was only one baby. The child appeared equidistant between the two of them.

The doctors, nurses, and medical staff admitted that no one was paying close attention to either of these deliveries. The mothers were R-o-b-u-s-t. Robust (also poor and uninsured).

It was clear after thorough medical examinations that both women had given birth and were no longer pregnant. The first woman said the child was ripped out of her. The other claimed one moment it was inside her, the next it was floating, bobbing up and down the hallway as if it was being carried away by an invisible current.

It is only fair, an attending physician said, *that each woman gets half of a baby.* He took scissors and cut the now squirming, squalling, infinitely pink creature in half. It was still. Color drained from both halves of the baby. *Walla.* Dead baby or babies. Depending on how you would use the plural in such a case.

Of course, my father was beside himself when his wife came home with only half an infant. He killed his wife, my mother, then. (whenever I ask him how he moved her from this world into the next, he says: *can't you see I did it out of love? I thought she had killed you, I would do anything for you*).

He threw my body on the fire and hours later removed a charred spinal cord. He took his wife's organs from her body and carefully arranged them to make a new daughter. He draped my mother's intestines around my throat, and I became beautiful, so beautiful in fact, he forgot to put the skin on.

Ichor

When I was a girl my nipples were hard enough to cut my hands—a point of pride.

Yet a day came when my body became vulnerable: my thighs turned into fontanels, which itched maddeningly during the transformation. I could feel the roots of three tongues forming in my throat. Ichor leaked between my legs, and the smell seemed to follow me everywhere. I furtively tried to sniff the other girls on this island to see if they were leaking the same substance. Once, I stole two pairs of underwear during gym class, but the stench was mine alone.

Not long after the transformation started, a woman appeared in my dreams.
I knew all the women and girls that lived on my island, but she was like no
other I had seen before. She had no lips (the sun made them rot—I knew this
instinctively), but her breath burrowed into my cochlea:

"My sons will tear into your body and come out with a fistful of jewels or
rotting fish spines (and when they are starving these will be more valuable
than gold). But you are a container to be unwrapped, pillaged, taken for
granted—nothing more."

I felt these words snake down into my cloaca and come to rest there. This was
how I first learned about the existence of men.

*

Here are my theories about men:

+ They grow thick horns that fracture their skulls. These horns might
have been evolutionarily advantageous eons ago, but now they're too
heavy to be useful. In fact, they're so heavy they cause men to sink
beneath the earth and that's why I have never seen them. Mother's
venture through a deep maze of caverns to find them, defeat them, and
create daughters.
+ Men arise from the sea, but only when the girls are in school. This
theory explains why the windows facing the ocean are all boarded up.
+ Men are made of sand. They could be lurking beneath my feet even
now.

*

I began to carry broken seashells in my pockets. Fantasized about driving their sharp edges into a man's throat. There was little resistance, the air filled with his blood mists. I imagined going to school the next day, triumphantly telling the other girls I was finally a woman. But those were daydreams, and in my dreams at night, my hand shook and when it shook, it wasn't strong enough to penetrate the man's skin. He hated me. In his eyes, I was no longer a daughter, but a lover. And he knew I could see him for what he was after all, he had been inside me, and I must have taken something from him, but what, what was it?

Did my classmates know men existed? Even while we braided dead fish in each other's hair, I was no longer able to relax beneath their touch. Either there was a horror in this world and they had no idea what awaited them, or they had known all along and kept it from me.

*

Outside of my dreams I met a man on the beach. And he said he smelled the dead fish my classmates braided in my hair, and that I didn't wash between my legs often enough—he could smell the ichor crusted on my thighs. When I reached for the seashell in my pocket it felt brittle, and I tried to stab him, but before I reached his throat, he snapped my wrist and it turned into sand. "You are mine," the man said.

*

And the only way I could escape was to transform into an animal, swim across oceans of time, space, spit, and algae. This is not a sad story.

Imagine for a moment:

The world melting away beneath your rasping, sandpaper tongue, layers
of skin falling away like clothes—yours and others—while your mucosa sings:
look at me, feel me—and yes, you know that death can come at any moment
(you are now an animal, now disposable), but every lover can be molded
into your desires, you lick away their shells until you find the parasites
beneath: children, infestations, universes: you dive
indiscriminately into them with your fangs.

SISTER::

I used to dream that my mother locked her lesser daughters
in a cage beneath my bed, I could hear them
gnawing on the bars. In some dreams, the lock would
pop open, and I swear I saw versions of myself appear from the darkness,
crawling on all fours. My mother, broom in hand, a vision of fierce domesticity,
would beat them back into submission.

:::STIISTER

After escaping, it took me six years to learn
how to write this letter:
"I will wear your skin & become you."

When I was 26, my mother's ghost took up occupancy in my bathtub.
She liked to complain about the eternal
burning of the afterlife—and claimed she could only be
soothed when her body was pressed against wet porcelain.
I would remind her that she didn't have a body,
she didn't have feelings. *You are such a vicious girl* (She didn't
say it—it had been said so often before).
I didn't mind her company, until the day she
protested my habit of plucking the hairs
from my labia, and leaving them scattered on the tile floor.
I turned the bathtub's faucet on and discovered the rush
of water broke her into pieces, and it took a long time, if not
longer, for her to coalesce again.
Slowly, I got the truth out of her:
"…I could give birth to an army of sons…
…but I could never give birth to another daughter…
…I knew you were the kind of woman who would devour other women…
….And yet, I only gave birth to baby girls…
…Even after my husband died…
…They seemed to spill out of my body…"
She tried to warn me about my sister, but
I turned on all the faucets in my home, and
vowed to keep them running. Even after my apartment flooded.

What I did not know how to write yet:
Yes, I burned the other daughters and our mother alive,
but only because I was determined to have you, the chosen daughter,
all for myself.
When you used to pee the bed, it would drip
through the mattress and fall on our heads.
I can still smell your urine in my hair,
feel the sensation of it running over my eyes and lips.

Yes, I had gotten rid of my mother's ghost, but I still had to contend
with the ghost of a sister, who was angry and very much not a ghost,
yet seemed to have vanished from the face of the earth.
I never knew why my mother chose me over her other daughters,
but it doesn't keep me from sleeping at night—it isn't my sin.
The only remarkable thing about me is that I have lots of lovers.
And when these men first enter my home
their worms are glistening and smug. They say things to me like:
"Your lovely rapids will be crammed with my corpses."
"I will tread you down to dust."
The men cannot even hear their worms,
though they lick their lips, and I imagine
their tongues are saying the very same things.

I first saw my sister lurking outside my apartment building.
I thought she was a stranger, brazenly seducing my lover,
but what did I care if this woman wanted my left overs?

I found sea slugs anonymously dropped off in front
of my apartment door. Some of them were dead by the time
I discovered the container, but others were
very much alive and I was sure, so sure, that they sighed
the same sigh as my lovers. I assumed the strange woman
had cursed them. But I didn't understand why
(had they been piss poor lovers?),
or why she entrusted them to me.

I started sleeping with your lovers.
I wanted to lick you off their skin/taste
your genetically superior fluids.
I thought if I swallowed enough of you
I would become you, the beloved, but there was never any of you left.

I turned my perpetually flooded apartment
into a giant saltwater aquarium by dumping
large discount containers of Morton's sea salt in my living room.

Eventually the strange woman started getting to the men first.
I didn't care about lipstick stains on my lover's cocks,
or that she burned her initials (which are the same as mine) on their
boar-hair bellies.
I used their penises as bottle openers or to scrub the dishes clean.
And when my lovers, tired, ask me if they can have what belongs to them back,
I say if you can find it, and achingly they search the house,
until they grab the wrong one (if they grab one at all) and scuttle out the door.
But then I knew this had nothing to do with the men.
This woman was trying to communicate with me, but why didn't she come out
and say it?

I kept writing letters, I stuffed them inside
sea slugs ordered from online (I made sure to choose
a variety of sea hares and nudibranchs).
I didn't trust the post office with my letters to you.
I thought for sure you would smash the slugs with
your hands (what I found beautiful, you would surely find
ugly) and find the letters inside.
Instead, you raised them as your children.

After years of watching you, I could predict the men you were going to bring
home.
I began seducing them first. I wanted to take anything I could away from you.

The stranger was me, I was her, we were blood, and I set out
into the world to find her.

I brought my sister home, even though she was feral around the edges. She
only tried to kill me three times. Sometimes, I found her curled up under my
bed, her face floating on the surface of the murky water. Her torso covered
in vibrantly colored nudibranchs.

Strangely we both plucked the hair from our labia with our fingers.
I call it a compulsion, she refers to it as a ceremony of existence.
She likes to watch the blood pool beneath the skin. And while I kept
this habit to the bathroom, she liked to do it while standing
stark naked in our living room. Her movements resembled a heron's—
meditative, precise.

It was my sister who hunted me down.
She cornered me in an elevator and twisted one of my nipples
until it popped, and bloomed into a girlish flower.
The petals a soft lavender, I was disgusted by how feminine it was.
I could not even name the names of any flowers.
It stood out against the fabric of my white shirt.
Did it press against the fabric until the shirt broke away from the skin?
Nonono, that isn't right, the petals pulled the fabric of my shirt toward them,
eating the cloth,
inserting it into a starfish mouth,
my shirt was disappearing,
the coffee stain from this morning already swallowed,
my fish belly exposed, the dipping scars looked like the outline of scales.

Our home was filled with a collection of sea slugs and phalluses.
You, sister, had one rule:
Never turn off the faucets.

Every Sunday, you brushed my hair. Just like our
mother used to brush yours—but I never remark on the coincidence.

It isn't until our fifth decade that I realize while my sister
had grown up near it, she had never really seen the ocean.
Unless she had stopped to gaze over the water while she burned
down the house—our mother and sisters with it—
even then, it had been dark, maybe even moonless.

When I see the ocean for the first time, I strip my clothes off.
I pluck the hair from my labia, you, with your superior lungs, try to shout
over the sound of the waves. But your voice falls dead on the sand.
"I am summoning the sea," I scream into the wind.
I watch your mouth wide crumble, teeth sink into an ocean liner, split your
bottom lips.
The next morning, we buy you dentures. I realize you are old before me.
You will die before me.

Decades later, long after my sister is dead, I go swimming
at another beach across the ocean, and I
find them. They burrow into my thighs, and I think I have been stung
by some rare, perhaps ancient
jellyfish. I think this while sitting in the waiting room of a foreign ER.
A surgeon removes white orbs from my
thighs, and I believe I have been inseminated by the rare,
ancient jellyfish. I trace the
tentacle pattern on my thighs, it is a message from the father,
I think, telling me how to raise his
children that would have been born if I had left well enough alone. But
I know nothing about children.
I am in my eighth decade.
"These are teeth," the surgeon says.
He drops them in the palm of my hand. I recognize them as yours,
smaller and eroded by salt. I
imagine these are your teeth's tender entrails/I move back
through time/you are a child and
asleep/and the teeth are in my fist/I shove them one by one
into your toothless gums/your
blood creeps into me.

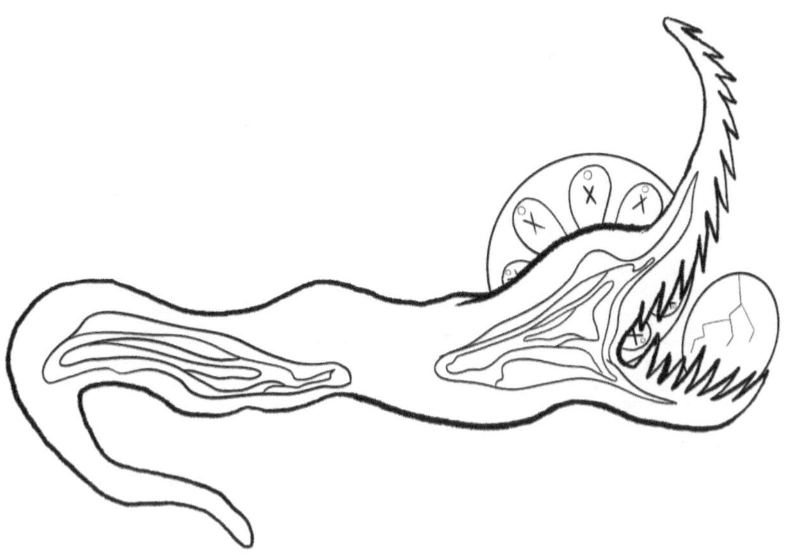

DADDY

My daughter laughs and points when I pick her up from preschool bare-breasted.

Her classmates laugh w/ her. She is powerful, that one.

Unlike my sons, she will one day abandon me, but have you seen the size of these TITS?

How could anyone abandon me?!?

From afar, they could be mistaken for the geothermal.

And at night, they even glow, but there's a simple explaining:

Sealed inside is an army of unconquerable suns. If I squeeze my breasts hard enough, you can see their light shining through the cracks of my nipples.

These suns are sons. My sons to be more specific.

A witch put a curse on me, on us.

She was tired of dealing with my fleshy progeny crusading on her front lawn.

After the curse, I was no longer the warlord I once was, and unfolded into the domestic life quite well.

My sons were not as lucky.

My daughter has never met her brothers.

She does not know I was once a fearsome warlord. She wipes her boogers on me without fear of decapitation.

Have you seen the size of these TIT HAIRS?

At home, my daughter draws a picture of my TITS hanging below my belly button. Then she draws a picture of my tits with a head of luscious hair sprouting from the rims, curling below my knees. She is inserting her own desires. My TIT HAIRS look nothing like this, We both know it, she is designing her own adult body.

During the night, she crawls into my bed, and fingers my fatty tissue. She says DADDY, it looks like spiders are stuck in your funnel cake, it looks like they are trying to unzip you. And it's true, they are exiting the universe of my body, hard & fast.

You probably think, these hairs could cut you, but no, no, no—

See it's all wrong. The hairs surrounding my nipples are quite soft, I will let you touch them (gentler than that please), if you promise not to tug.

After I bathe, they are as soft as horseshoe crabs.

I have to braid the TIT HAIRS together, coat them in a special potion (recipe: an ancient lover's cum—distilled, two fetid lambs' tails, gelatin, gun powder) to give them any chance against my daughter. She is ravenous for my TITS, and when she suckles, light spills from my sons into her mouth. Later, I have to pick out the yellow gunk that gets stunk b/t her teeth.

In that first phone call, when I told my mother I was no longer a warlord, she instructed me to cut off my breasts and place them in the bathtub.

"My sons will die," I said.

"You will be a warlord again. You can impregnate entire continents." I could hear her, foaming at the mouth. I knew soon, she would drown in it.

A Horse Lover

I fell in love w/ a Carnivorous Horse.

I had no tongue.

I cannot remember if I lost it before or after I met her. The stitches never melted away, and I felt them digging into surrounding soft tissue. At night, they would even begin to chew.
Now you will understand, nothing surprises me.

On our third date, the horse devoured a breast of mine (a beast of mine).
When I didn't moan in pleasure my horse's teeth became inflamed w/ wine & fruit. She latched onto the inside of my thighs w/ a proboscis
drank any sustenance I had left.

There was no milk for my children.

I mashed up pieces of my own flesh to feed them. "meat, meat, meat, meat," the lil sociopath's chanted.
It made me sick and to this day, I don't know if they're alive or dead. What I mean is: I've never found their remains. There were so many nights where I

dreamed, yes dreamed, with my eyes wide open,

the Carnivorous Horse licking their skulls clean.

I never knew what made me different than the men, women, and children she devoured. I spent my nights inside her mouth. Once I found an eye stuck b/t her teeth—the pupil's mouth gaping. I stored it underneath my remaining breast, until it began to stink, and the Carnivorous horse fished it out w/ her tongue. I shivered in pleasure.

At night, I soaked my hair in a concoction of bird's milk and honey, and she would watch with what must have been adoration, as I slowly plaited it into a single braid. She liked when I used the ends of my hair to tickle her lips & the soft skin around her nostrils. I could forget—at least for a time—that she was the Carnivorous Horse, who trampled entire villages (including all I had ever known) beneath her hooves. We were merely lovers.

Why are you called the Carnivorous Horse?

I couldn't ask of course,

       I had no tongue,

            but my whole body screamed the

question.

"After I ate my father," the Carnivorous Horse said. "I was known as the patricidal horse, until I ate the next year's homecoming queen. I got blood on my sea foam colored suit, then the title 'Carnivorous Horse' fit best."

Soon after, in the hours of the early morning, I swear I could hear sobs coming from the pit of my lover's belly, and I wondered if those were horse's tears. Yet I had my doubts:

    a) I had never heard my Carnivorous Horse cry, nor had she ever shed a single tear in my presence.
    b) I had never seen any horses cry, either in movies or in real life. They were unbelievably stoic creatures.

How does one eat a homecoming queen anyway?
Did my horse lover leap onto the stage, as the queen was being crowned, and devour her—tiara and all?

Or did she wait until the homecoming queen snuck into the bathroom to surreptitiously drink from a flask?
….were they lovers?

One night, I tied my braid around one of the Carnivorous Horse's thirty-six incisors, and tickled her throat until she was compelled to swallow me.

I landed on a homecoming queen, I could tell by the neon-blue mascara staining the hair under her lower lashes.

"I've been listening to your god-awful moaning for years," she said.
"What did she see in you?"
I couldn't say anything. I had no tongue.
"Will you at least help me fix my dress. My mother sewed it for me. A

herculean effort as you can see."

She clacked her hooves together.

The dress was embroidered with pearls and shells I had never seen before. Even in this low light, it mimicked water & algae rising to my ankles, then swirling to my hips. It would not be long before I was completely submerged. I plucked out strands of my hair to use as thread, and one by one my rope, and life, unraveled.

We had centuries to get to know each other in the stomach of the Carnivorous Horse.

The homecoming queen tried to fashion me a tongue, even chewing off the tip of her own. But it was a useless contraption that felt awkward in my mouth.

I fixed her makeup. She clipped off some of her eyelashes to weave into my own.

My hair grew back, thicker than ever, and stretched through the membranes of the Carnivorous Horse's internal organs & the pores of her skin. One day, her body cracked open. She had been reduced to a dehydrated husk—long ago strangled by my hair. We climbed out into a new world w/o horses or humans.

The homecoming queen and I are growing old together (we are already old, but older still). We are not lovers, merely friends, and each night we crown each other homecoming queens of the universe.

Dawn Speaks:

My mother's last memory is my first. I cannot tell you what has always been mine. With her final breath (did she have lungs? I do not know her species) it transferred to me:

Once I saw a woman,

Once I saw a woman swim up to my island (I had never seen a human before, it was their first year in existence), dripping skinned-knees-on-asphalt, a color so pink I wanted to lick it off, and chew the small stones clinging to her skin b/t my molars. She slowly unhooked her bra, but instead of her breasts slipping to the earth, it was my eyes that fell out of my skull

and the dirt came up to meet them. My eyes rolled to separate ends of the earth, and I hatched from one of these mammalian eggs: boneless & breathless (I think this is when the memory becomes my own). I have never met whoever hatched from the other eye, lovers have told me somewhere on this earth I have a brother, (but he is still bloodless). I disappear whenever the sun blazes full in the sky, and I only return to existence when night recedes.

*

Every new day vessels of men wash up on my island.

Some I take for lovers.

*

I am never bored by a body. I can talk to a creature who occupies a body for days & days, until it turns to detritus and is blown off my island or carried away by vicious birds.

After a millennium of wanting, I created mine through pure desire, and the gods told me, as I was growing the roots of my tongue, still unable to speak or lash back, I was the only creature who had fucked her being into existence. And they trapped me here, on my island, but I had never thought of leaving, even before then.

Yet I built myself wrong.

My first body was a giant pink terracotta rectangle.

And I still haven't gotten it quite right:

Today there are sea anemones in my belly, their spines have shredded intestines, and are bursting through my abdominal wall. From afar it looks like there is a line of thick hair rippling in the breeze.

I have feathers, talons, claws, and a split tongue.

I'm always bleeding between my legs, and the blood gets caught underneath my fingernails. It refuses to wash away, and drenches everything I touch, including the sky.

And still when the sun blazes, this body will disappear. Every new day I must rebuild from scratch.

*

I don't know where these men come from, what calls them to the edge of the Earth.

At the beginning of human existence, women also came to my island.

They do not come here anymore. I don't know if the gods or their men have kept them away.

I would split the women in two to learn how to make a body.

Some have wombs eating away at their lungs, others are pure soul and viscera.

Mostly, their bodies are like my island, filled with sand, soil, water, trees, and rotating moons.

Sweeping winds move currents of blood to each limb. A kleitoris winds its way through a forest to the roof of her mouth, where it resides like a beloved pet. Or it slithers through her body like a weasel, chewing on the edges of her nerves. Carving her fingers down to claws, her spine into a bow.

And of course, each body has birds pecking away at the integrity of the cell.

*

I used to talk to the women as I examined and rummaged through the contents of their bodies.

They are not like me. They do not want a body. They tell me they want to fuck (or be fucked) so hard they lose their body and do not need to eat, sleep, or shit. OR better yet, they want to not care if they shit, and it consumes their lovers & children entirely.

When I tell them about the birds inside their bodies they do not believe me.

*

I have loved the men who come off the vessels too, but it is not the same—

I do not have the urge to cut them open and model my own being after theirs.

I have seen the world end many times now, and it is always on the wing of birds. In some endings, it is the birds inside the bodies that strike first—they boil collagen, simmer bones into a paste. Other times, they drown mortals in bird cum and feathers that rain down from the heavens.

*

But this, this is the ending that I have lived most often:

I'm alone on my island, vessels of men no longer arrive on my shores. I'm alone in blood stained floral underwear, and birds fly up to my window (I built a house just to get away from them) they have the eyes of my ex-loves jiggling in their sockets, and yet, there is no flicker of recognition.

Then I disappear—and there is nothingness, truly nothing—until night gives way.

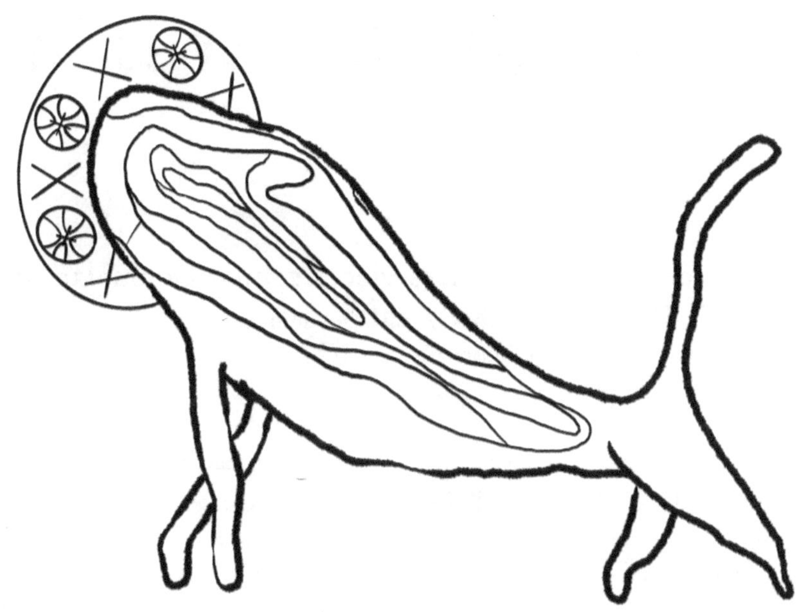

My Dead Mother is into F

**My mother is a limbless electric blue amphibian and
when I'm just a baby, I eat** her skin clean off. It regrows every
three days, but the neighbors are tired of the   , so one
day she disappears.

Because my mother is an electric blue amphibian, I am half eclectic—
baptized in a tub of fresh kills (or was it fish skulls or fiscals?)

They entered through every hole I possessed & to this day I am terrified
by the way my body opens and closes under water. I've never gotten the
smell of rotting flesh out of my ears, and for years, I couldn't masturbate
w/o scales and ligaments climbing into my hands, burrowing beneath my
fingernails. During school, I couldn't stop sniffing them because I knew the
smell was there, and everyone could tell what I had done.

My mother is a limbless

electric blue

and I marry a man who is aroused by transformations of all kinds— w/ time,
and careful scientific observation, he discovers that he can manipulate them.
He cuts me in my sleep,

Rotting Fish & Crystals

and another woman emerges from the hole.

She has my eyes.

He watches her ass bounce, thighs tremble. A line of perspiration ruining her shorts. (My copycats and I emit a peculiar smell, it is impossible to wash away our stench, and it is contained within every liquid molecule).

She only lives for a few days, and my husband becomes accustomed to the taste of skin. Unlike mine, theirs cannot grow back. Instead they scab over. My husband leaves them for dead, and I'm jealous, so jealous, but after the first few die, I rub ointment on their wounds.

The scabs are brittle and hard and grow over their eyes even.

I lie, and tell the girls their scabs look like fish scales.

They grope their bodies up and down. They grope each other.

I remember what it is like to be in adolescence. But the girls emerged as women—and to the world—even to me—their innocence is unholy.

"You lied to us." "It's all one piece."

"It's true," I say, making the words up as they come. "You are each a single scale. I am going to sew us together into a giant fish and we will swim away from here.... I will be your eyes if you let me."

In my dreams meat hooks hang from my mother's clavicles. I can hear her tongue flickering against hollow, back-facing teeth. A limping chant escapes from her lips: "pistel," "crystal," and "distal."

She lived long before humans were ever born, but died only five years after marrying one.

What is the relationship b/t the formation of a flower to her death?

Will the answer make me grieve just enough, so I can be happy?

In my dreams, she is alive and I'm dead. Horse before the cart.

I cannot protect my copy cats, I'm not sure that I even want to.

I am always sleeping—it's the caecilian part of my brain—but I do not know what happens in my own house.

In a dream, my copycats eat my skin, and although mine can grow back, they don't know when to stop, or more likely, they won't stop. I vanish—not even my blood remains on their fingertips.

Should I decide whether it's my sisters or daughters he's fucking?

Is it obvious?

I built a subterranean fortress to store my copycats. There are hundreds now. My mother had no legs. I do not know how my parents made love, but years after her death one of my neighbors invited me into his home. His breath smelled like overripe fruit & medicine. I felt it infect the air and weave around my body, until fermentation set in. I couldn't move, and he told me a story.

He saw my parents together in the fields. He saw my mother wrap her body around my father, who was completely enveloped by his wife, her body pulsing.

He then held a knife to my throat.

"Show me if you are anything like your mother."

I do not want to tell you this story, instead I want to tell you a story about wolves. But there is no time.

I often dream about wolves and their ever-changing eyes. Those eyes are my eyes. Or they belong to my sister-daughters, the living and the dead. Sometimes I dream that the wolves give us their eyes, stick them in our empty sockets. Lick our cheeks, and say, you are an animal.

I dream that we see my husband for who he is. We shove crystals then flowers   then dead fish   down his throat.

When I enter the subterranean fortress for the last time (though I do not know it is the last), the girls are sewing themselves together, each forming a single scale. They are silent when I approach. And I know, I know they want nothing to do with my eyes.
In another dream, my mother said, "if only you learned how to smell you

would have survived."

And she asks me what scent is hanging in the air, and I know,

she wants me to say, "I can smell the dreams of dead people in the river."
"And they're still drowning."
"They don't even know it's over yet."

Instead, I say, "wet rocks."

In my dream, this happens only a few days before she disappears, but it
could have happened years earlier. Was I ever born?

Transubstantiation

At night, a young priest crawls through my window.
He brings with him what I think is the smell of the catechism. My naïveté
is forgivable, this is my first love and it consumes me. All day, I could think
of nothing else besides my young priest.

The young priest is a holy being.

He presses his face into my neck. I take his fingers in mine and snap them off.
He cries only a little, my throat itches from his tears. But thank goodness,
my father does not hear.

I put the young priest's fingers inside me. I'm a virgin, and it hurts, but I moan anyway.

I'm proud of myself for knowing this is how a woman behaves when she has a lover. Even if a lover is meant to be a secret, the moans must still be performed. (If a woman doesn't perform the moans, it is simple really, a lover will not love her).

We will never be apart, I tell him. The priest emits a small vaporous cloud of piss.

I'm stunned by the realization that he doesn't know my thoughts, that my desire isn't strong enough to transmute flesh, but I know that if my thoughts could somehow become his, he would understand.

I tell him a story:

Today I was rubbing my nipples through my shirt, while staring at the sea. The young priest interrupts me, you live nowhere near the sea. I tell him that it is dark out. You have to listen.

I thought, what if you died in a car wreck, and I never knew about it? After all, you are Catholic, and my family is Episcopalian. (I am a liar— there is no religion on my birth certificate).

And the sensation of cotton creating micro-tears in the delicate tissue of my breasts made me lonely. (I am prone to depressive episodes, this I do not tell him).

In the morning, I discover that droplets of my young priest's finger-blood

*I would have no reason to
heat of your death. Now, I
do. Only at the moment of
your demise will your fingers
begin to disintegrate inside
me.*

*I will tell everyone, I have
bacterial vaginosis, when
they inevitably ask, 'What
is that smell?'*

*There is only one regret— if
I wasn't a virgin, I could fit
all of you inside me.*

have leaked into my underwear.

The finger-blood is a completely different shade of red than my menstruation, thus incriminating.

In my bedroom is a geological formation (i.e. a laundry basket)—complete with river silt and a lava bed. I ball the underwear up tightly and bury it for safekeeping in one of the middle strata, which is composed of heavier particles of sedimentation.

When I return home from school I find the molecular composition of my bedroom has changed. And I know that my mother has stolen the dirty underwear from my laundry basket. Her nose is magnificent.

I should have known this would happen, but I had no idea that she even knew what a priest smelled like.

And I become so certain that I will find my mother in the kitchen glowing with the bioluminescence of Christ himself, that I am afraid to ever leave my bedroom again (even though I can longer stand the smell). My father knocks on my door after midnight and coldly informs me that my mother has stuffed my underwear down her dying father's throat. Since he now has a holy artifact in his possession, he can finally die.

But my grandfather is not a member of the church, so the whole family drives hours in the middle of the night to dump his body in the gulf. My mother coos motherly to my little sisters, and only refers to me as an apparition.

My grandfather's body is in the fetal position behind the last row of seats. I
did not know it was possible to bend a corpse in this manner. I can see the
shape of his foot beneath the bed sheet. And if it wasn't for this foot being
definitively foot-shaped, I could pretend that we were transporting a giant
snail back to its natural habitat. But he is human, and he is dead, and my
mother is making it very clear that I am dead to her as well. Years in the future,
when I dream of this trip, I am underneath the sheet too. Sometimes my
arms are stiff and I can't reach an itch on my calf. The itching is consumptive.
It is the feeling of my skin celebrating a divorce from muscle and fat. In other
dreams, my arms creep like a vine around my grandfather's torso. The vine
keeps growing, until our bodies disappear, the backseat covered in foliage.
I can't see, but I can feel the vines growing, they are covered in my skin. I
even feel them as they grow through my sisters' and father's bodies, exit like
waterfalls through their eyes and mouths. My mother seems immune to my
rampant overgrowth. She never stops driving the car.

In happier dreams, I am just a shell on my grandfather's back. Our human
lives a momentary mistake in our existence.

After the funeral, my mother returns the underwear. I find them folded
nicely in my top drawer, still hardened with saltwater and phlegm. Slowly,
the rest of my underwear goes missing. My mother has used dynamite to
destroy the geological formation in my bedroom. There's nothing left.

One day, I wear the underwear to school. It is my only pair.

It is a Tuesday.
I can feel my grandfather stirring in the cells of the fabric. His breath

moistens my lips. I do not blame him for refusing to remain in the ocean with his corpse. The gulf is slick with the dead. I am not sure if it is guilt or resignation, but I do not resist when I feel myself inflate like a balloon.

His spirit plunges into my body during my afternoon pre-calculus class. With my young priest's fingers still firm inside me, and the spirit of my grandfather occupying my womb, I no longer feel insatiable lust. I am finally cured of my womanly condition.

I am brought to the nunnery on my seventeenth birthday. My mother asks them to perform the blood test. The nuns hold me down and jab a needle through my clavicle. Our family name is entered into a registry. My siblings are too young to understand the significance of this moment. My mother has forgiven me—now when the time comes, we can all be buried in a nice cemetery. I bet it will be one of those rich people cemeteries, on a cliff, overlooking the Atlantic Ocean.

The sisters inform me I am to serve in one of their holy wars. And my mother once again proves herself magnificent. She doesn't even look me in the eyes—the eyes of her firstborn—while the whole family climbs back into the minivan.

I never see them again.

*

I am in my seventh decade now, and have become an artist of moderate renown. Critics associated with the church, celebrate my work: they say I have perfectly captured the non-erotic female gaze. I paint only portraits of the young priest, whose fingers are still firm inside me, from memory alone.

A reputation for serenity precedes me.

The younger sisters seek my counsel. They speak of an insatiable hunger, which I barely remember. I tell them to fill their bodies with sea shells and rocks. If that is not enough, I help them fill every hole with cement. In the most desperate cases, we sneak out of the convent at night and travel to the sea. I instruct the girls to prostrate themselves on the sand.

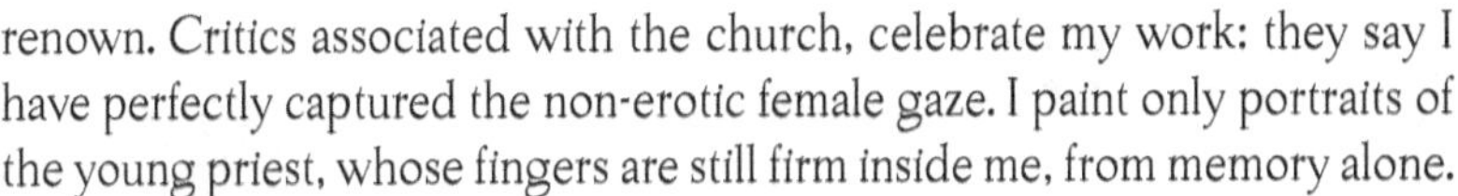

Diagnosis

There are numerals in my mouth. They hold their breath
and mine. They are entirely dependent on the birth of my dead sister's dead
daughter's child. If this child survives, it will climb its way out of
bodies (out of bodies), out of coffins (out of coffins), out of soil (out of soil),
out of stone (out of stone), out of ornamental grass, well-maintained grass,
existential grass (is more human than plant by now)(unable to communicate
with its kind for a millenia)(resented)(a scapegoat)(we are all so tired of
living this way)(but especially the grass).

When the child arrives it's fingernails won't drip blood on the carpet. They
will have evaporated (so to the fingerbones). They will have done more
work than I have in my entire life (I cannot even be bothered to wash myself)
(my hair leaves stains on the fabric of my couch (of any couch really)).

The numerals are responsible for my bad teeth. My crooked teeth. My too-
many teeth.

The numerals whisper this truth into the holes in my chest:

If the child arrives, the numerals will disappear. They will become the
child's missing fingernails.
I will not see the numerals again. At least, not very often.

The child will not want me as a parent.

When my sister was alive, she did not want me as a sister or a brother.

She said that I lacked the "aliveness" (read: sumptuousness, viciousness) required of human beings to survive the decade. (There was talk of dimming the sun. We turned our enthusiasm to smaller orbiting bodies).

The numerals say there are realms (a few, not as many as you may think). The numerals say that in those realms it is different from here. My sister never descends beneath the earth, and when her daughter is born, the daughter lives. It is so easy. The daughter betrays her inherited biome. She is like warm soft bread, beloved by all the loving. Except for me. She doesn't betray that part of her lineage.

She doesn't like that I let grass grow on my back, that I paint it Scheele's Green like my masculine ideal (Napoleon). That I insert stalks into my pores. That when I get out of the shower and shake myself dry, it rains soil. (Grass is a soulless creature)(made even more soulless by these machinations).

And in the other realms where my sister does descend below the earth, her daughter is born a decade later. I do not know what that birth was like. The daughter manages to claw past a layer of coffins (crushed and clotted), past the bodies that were intended for the coffins but rebelled, (now they kiss everyone and all their parts). Then she pulls apart layers of clay and soil. I like to imagine she is swimming through all our filth and all our sins, long hair billowing & uncut just like her foreskin (which envelopes her entire body)—it is a journey that takes years. When she rests she eats boar sausage and gooseneck (given to her by medieval Christian pilgrims that died long ago)(who have no interest in staying in their graves or beds)(or abiding continental curfews)(and no interest in returning to the surface).

Traveling is exhaustive and doesn't agree with her internal organs. Every bowel movement is a triumph. In the future, her shit will be excavated and interred in museums for the wealthy to look at. (Very few patrons will be permitted to smell these remains)(Their nostrils will never return to their original shape)

But no, this never occurs here (in this realm she stays in her mother's coffin, and never tries goose or sausage). Still, even when she joins the realm of the living, the numerals inform me we live apart. She has no hands. We hardly speak on the telephone or via email. So, I suspect, this child will want nothing to do with me either. (Animosity bred in the grave)(animosity that hydrates the skin)(luminous)(luminous)

But the numerals say if the child appears, they will become her fingernails (so to the fingerbones). They will weave themselves into new kinds of tissue. I think they are excited by the possibility. It is all they can talk about (therefore it is all I can write about).

I'm hurt preemptively by my nearest kin's betrayal. I'm preemptively wallowing, preemptively longing, preemptively locking the door.

But after the numerals leave, I can go on dates again.

As of now, I am a sexual pariah. Even when I lay my eggs in remote corners of this town (far, far from my apartment I assure you), no one will fertilize them. I think they can tell they are mine. My eggs have always been uniquely dispirited. And the thought of my mouth is enough to make any pollinator vomit and sweat past the point of capable performance.

I have never been interested in mating like an insect. I want to rut like an equinox (some cloven thing), forgotten by humans in the Exclusion Zone. But these teeth, these teeth! (I mean, anti-teeth) (Illusory teeth) numerals go away pls! (No, come back)(backtome)(stitch yourself to the hard parts of my mouth)(bark like a dog)(whisper your secrets into the holes in my chest)(I cut off my breasts, you were my only witness)(we will never leave this apartment)(help me cut them off again).

So, It does not matter if my sister's daughter's child will not take to me.

I can maybe have my own child, if the numerals go away.

To the untrained eye, the numerals in my mouth resemble teeth, and humans stopped having teeth in their mouth two centuries ago. It didn't happen gradually like you might think. Just like that, our teeth were gone.

Stage Directions: Turn around and face the ghosts who have been reading over your shoulder. You become suspicious of how these ghosts digest time. You become suspicious of the number three. You become suspicious of your sister, even though she is still alive (and in braces). You notice these ghosts have no teeth. You become too aware of yourself. Your teeth are very large like swollen white plates. You ask the ghosts to remove them by tapping on your left front tooth. rap-tap-tap. The sound is crisp and a little wet. The ghosts nod their heads. They oblige.

I swear I hear her loud as a cicada. She is coming now. Out of coffins (out of coffins), out of soil (out of soil), out of stone (out of stone),

wretching

at the smell of grass.

Vulvodynia

I am the mother of seven sons, but before I give birth to seven sons, I must conceive seven sons.

My perineum is blissful. My perineum is dead. My perineum is chock-full of crocuses and hyacinth. I used to cull these flowers from my flesh with deadly precision then send them off to a laboratory for testing. Now, I let them grow. It is too painful otherwise, and the tests were always inconclusive. On a molecular level, the skin cells clinging to the flowers are too disruptive.

*

The flowers run in the blood:

Rose petals grew on my sister's back, from far away she looked like a salmon, who moments before you found her, had grown legs and walked out of the river. But she died when she was only twelve and I was younger. Our mother always thought she would be murdered. *There are so many murderers in this world,* she told us. We thought one would capture her and rip the petals off, leaving her to bleed to death in the dirt. My mother and I would fantasize about it when she wasn't there, in a terrified sort of way. *It will happen when I am late to pick her up from school, she said. Yes, when there is too much traffic.*

A murderer will lure her away.

And I imagined that the murderer would have to be very handsome to trick my sister, because not only was she beautiful, but she was clever too. Then the fantasies would be interrupted by jealousy, which I will always associate with the changing of seasons in my internal biome, like suddenly it was snowing in my stomach, and I couldn't get warm because the cold came from inside.

Why was the handsome murderer not interested in murdering me?

But my sister died in the night—it was her gallbladder they said. And the smell of roses disappeared from our town for twenty-five years. And the smell of tire factories, and rotting fish on the shore, and the piles of sulfur, and even the stench of our own sweat, rolled in to take her place. We had become so used to her scent that it had become all-consuming and imperceptible.

The realizations, of course, did not happen overnight.

A few weeks after my sister died, we learned we had no idea how to cook. All the freshwater had possessed the fragrance of rose, which in turn infused the delicate flaky morsels of fish that composed our every meal.

There were more dire consequences: we realized the milk we were drinking was often sour, we weren't attracted to our lovers (maybe we never were), and bathing was more complicated than we could have ever imagined.

After my sister died, my mother grew mean. Or maybe she was always mean. What I mean is, she once told me I was lucky that my sister was dead. Now there was a chance that someone on this great green earth could love me. While my sister was alive, I was doomed to have lovers that lusted after something—no *someone*—more.

*

I am the mother of seven sons, but before I give birth to seven sons, I must conceive seven sons.

This is not an easy task.

With each new lover, my skin cells splinter and fester. And they're either too lazy, or don't understand how to put themselves back together.

I am surprised it doesn't all come apart, my insides spilling on a lover's phallus. Maybe it will any day now.

It's strange, I can still remember their insults (intentional or otherwise):

You are a pile of somethin' worm-eaten,

Your vestibule resembles a raft of enflamed tax documents,

The center of your cunt looks like a fat and juicy spider. She's staring at me,

etc, etc, etc.

I can even remember the peculiarities of my lovers' voices, the way they held their saliva in their mouth (do they let it pool behind their teeth or under their tongue?), but for the life of me, I can't remember their hair color or how they died years later.

Does it matter? Like almost everyone, they were probably murdered.
And it is strange—

I can't remember a thing my dead sister said to me. Not a single phrase.

Only one lover, the GEOLOGIST, got it right: *the lower half of your body is a complex system of underwater caverns and caves.*

Essentially, what he was saying was that the flowers growing from my body were the least of my problems.

*

I've given birth to seven sons, but each son, the moment after he was born, discovered he had legs to walk on and I was too exhausted to stop him from wandering back inside me. My sons never come out again. But I know they're alive, because they eat and I feel it. And they pass waste and grow and play games and I feel all of that too. And everything they produce inside me must also leave my body.

The first time I soiled myself in public, it was on my younger sister's wedding day (born to replace the dead). I ruined the carpet of the chapel, the hem of the wedding gown—a dress that had been passed down through the generations. My mother was so embarrassed she couldn't look me in the face. She took only one picture. It was of her foot, joints swollen, toes curled in anxiety, a small lake of shit swirling underneath.

*

The GEOLOGIST helped me map my terrain using government-funded stealth technology. There is a large river inside me. A not-so-impressive mountain range. Several distinct biomes.

If only we could communicate with your seven sons, imagine all of the species we could discover. I forbade it. Then one day, the GEOLOGIST was murdered.

There are so many murderers in this world, I wonder when will we run out of the living?

One of my sons is very thoughtful. He sits at the top of a glacier, the source of my river.

Sometimes the river changes direction and exits out of a new hole in my body. This son plucks my favorite species of flower and he fills the water with their petals and stems (he lightly chews on them to bring about their scent) and when I wake up to their fragrance I know that once again the river has changed directions. I must quickly find my new mouth to avoid drowning my community. I have lost several neighbors and cats to this fate.

Tell me, does any other woman in the world have such a gracious child?

I am the mother of seven sons, but before I give birth to seven sons, I must conceive seven sons.

The first time it happened, I was ten years old. I was friends with a girl who had the most beautiful andelongated tailbone in town. Her mother spent many hours of her life peeling away the flesh and carving intricate symbols into the vertebrae, even while her daughter screamed. Every night her voice grew louder and louder until all the dogs in town ran away. And for a while, the murderers ran away too, but later they returned with sharper claws and stronger teeth.

My mother warned me about the girl, *you vanish when you are near her. I can't even see you and I'm your mother.*

One night the girl with the elongated tailbone and I went to the house of a boy I liked. My friend and the boy disappeared behind a bedroom door, while I remained alone in the kitchen, grimacing and sipping on a bottle I had explicitly been told not to touch.

She told me later she had to get up several times to pee while they made love. He kept begging her to hold it inside, so he could finish.

But that night, I didn't know. I didn't know any of this. I wished a murderer would break into the house and gobble them up. And I cried for having such a terrible thought. Then I cried because I remembered my dead sister's funeral. When I am sad, I feel all the sadness my body has ever felt at once. When I was younger, I thought this was unique to me. And while I was still crying, the boy returned to the kitchen. He asked me what was wrong, and I tried to describe the complexity of feeling multiple sadnesses at once, when all your bad memories decide to be remembered at the same time. The boy stuck his thingie quickly inside me, before I even had time to know if I needed to pee or not (although when I told this story to my friend with the elongated tailbone, I think I told her the urge was unbearable and we cried together over our swollen urethras, holding and stroking them in our hands).

This is how my first son was conceived. But I would hold him high up in my body for years to come.

*

I am the mother of seven sons, but before I give birth to seven sons, I must conceive seven sons....

When I was thirteen, I dared to look upon a man as old as my father, and when he slapped me I didn't look away. He made his daughters watch as he hit me again, and still, I did not look away. How lucky it must be to be a father with no sons and only daughters! When he saw that they did not flinch or shy away from the violence, he kept hitting me until the whole family was vibrating from sexual excitement.

They took me away and locked me in their basement. The father forced everyone in the family to pee in jars. He kept these jars on long shelves that lined the basement walls. Each jar was labeled with a peculiar series of letters and numbers. Only in his obituary, which I read many years later, did I learn that he was considered a great mind. A man determined to bridge the gap between the sciences and arts by collecting every known shade of yellow that the human body was capable of producing. But I didn't know that then. I only wanted death. Every night when the house went dark, the jars seemed to glow.

He made sure to display them in a way that made them seem not perverse, but rather a collection artfully arranged. It was hard to look away. One night, I unscrewed the lid off of each jar, took a sip, then smashed it on the ground. I let their contents fill my body with warmth and light. Soon there was a flood. A wave of urine erased most of the town, including the university where he taught. For a while, their house bobbed along with the fast-moving currents, but then it sank. I do not remember how I survived and the family didn't—there was no way for me to unlock that basement, but the facts are I did survive and then some.

*

And the third time happened like this: when I was five my mother mistook a coyote for a lost dog (this was before they had all vanished). She coaxed it into the back of her car, where it sat right next to me.

Outside the car, the coyote was suspicious and lurking, and I could see thousands of years of malice against my species in its eyes. Inside the car, it panted like any other dog, although I swear to this day, its tongue was a few centimeters longer than is appropriate for polite company. A stranger pulled over to tell my mother what she had done (luckily, he was not a murderer). But it was still too late, and I was already pregnant with my third child. At the time, I was only eight years old. If you have learned anything about the world from this story, it's that conception cannot and will not occur in a linear manner.

*

The fourth time, I was lucky enough to have fallen in love. And I bit the tip of my lover's tongue off, (I think I must have been thinking about the coyote). I was surprised when she impregnated me. She was very proud that she had impregnated me, and I felt betrayed by her pride. Naturally, we drifted apart.

She died before I ever gave birth. The ferocity of my love for her seems childlike now. I dreamt the wet parts of our eyes would touch. That our eyelashes would fuse together, and I shuddered in my sleep from this simple action.

When I first had my period, I was ashamed. I hid the blood-soaked rags underneath my mattress and what sprouted was a very strange mammal of a tree. The bark was covered in fur, and its branches sprouted hair, fingernails, sometimes claws. I nicknamed the tree, "My Lioness." She was fierce and soft. She grew straight through my chest, the roof of our house, then turned towards the sea. My father cut her down, but he left behind a single shred of fur-covered bark in my body. From this grew an embryo.

This happened when I was only four years of age.

*

One of my sons chewed off his hands while he was in the process of being born. And in that way, he created another son.

One time I masturbated.

One time I saved a baby bird.

One time that baby bird died in a bowl I placed on the kitchen table. I forgot about it, but the cat didn't.

I am nearly in my eight decade, but I look much older. I like to write in very public spaces. I know you are just as likely to be murdered in plain sight, but it makes me feel safer. Somehow having witnesses to my murder makes it seem not as bad.

My eyes are borrowed from an even older body. They are disintegrating faster than the rest of me. I cannot afford new ones.

Imagine seeing a small woman (from faraway I am often mistaken for a child) type in very large letters:

ONE TIME I MASTURBATED
ONE TIME I SAVED A BABY BIRD

What would you think?

I cannot be the only person on this earth who gets a tingle on the back of her neck from spying on strangers. But what would you think if you saw these phrases right next to one another? What would a baby bird come to mean in this case? I would assume it was code or antiquated slang. I would think the old woman in front of me was talking about a scrotum or the head of a penis or perhaps snidely remarking on the underdeveloped-but-already-gently-sagging breast of her great granddaughter.

But no, what I mean is what I meant: I saved a baby bird. I was so proud of myself (except in the instance, which occurs half of the time, where the baby bird eventually dies, in the other cases, the baby bird is eternal). I usually kill things. For instance, I accidentally killed my parents. But I really did save the baby bird, even before it died, if it died, I saved it from a previous death that hunted it and delivered it to a new one. And at least this one occurred in the privacy of an air-conditioned home.

But it was the pride in saving the baby bird that doomed me and got me pregnant.

The rest of the children were fathered under normal circumstance, that is I am an adult woman who knows better, yet even in my seventies, I still refuse to use a condom.

I cannot wait to father a collection of children, who will be detached from the recesses of my body.

One time I fathered a complete set of dining room furniture, but this is not the same thing. The flowers run in the blood, and I believe they want it this way. I am envious of the sexually-deviant professor & his bouquet of daughters. Even if they are all dead.

If only I could stop having sex.

My labia are swollen and painful and still I have sex and I don't know why.

And my gynecologist insists on plucking the hyacinth and crocus stems growing from my perineum and yet it does nothing, nothing, *it does nothing*. But the flowers look nice next to the examination table. Except, for when I visit the doctor, my body is allowed to grow wild.

If I don't have sex, I feel the holes in my body shrinking. And I'm afraid that the seven sons inside me will suffocate.

I am tired of finding their defecations smeared on my thighs, and sometimes I want them to die, but not like that.

When I stop having sex my pimples disappear and then the pores themselves. Strangers tell me how beautiful I am. Next my anus evaporates. One of my lovers told me that it looked just like the condensation of water on an air conditioning unit. *The height of femininity.*

My labia are swollen and painful and still I have sex;
and I don't know why.

It is written, that the person who first discovered magic was Zoroaster, king of the Bactrians. Like me, he was perpetually pregnant and found himself incapable of fathering a child. There is a story that he released a feral horde of birds inside his body to drag his children out into the world, to prove that he had an heir. But they chose to let the birds peck out their eyes rather than join their parent in his kingdom.

I do not know if there is a connection between the magic and the pregnancies, the lost children, and the desire to father a child—it is a nice thought. Like me, it is written that Zoroaster had fragile skin.

The skin between his legs often tore in new and exciting ways. While riding into a battle a hole opened up in his flesh. 200 men and their horses disappeared from the face of the earth. Zoroaster returned, alone, naked, and on foot.

THE
CONN
OISSEUR

He inserts his cock into my ass,
and there is a sensation.

iiiiiiiiiiiiii am not a boneless, just feral.

There are many types of sensations.

iiiiiiiiiiii am not a connoisseur.

He inserts his cock into my ass,
And we both wait for the fifth and final coming of the
savior.

Flood waters swirl around my hands and knees.
My lips form a soft O. A swarm of cockroaches (an
ancient and noble species, from which EYE am
descended) pours forth from my mouth. They
drip infectious agents into the water, polluting our
bodies, we are stuck to this mattress for all eternity,
your cock still inside me. It is like a trapped animal,
it thrashes and bites me, and you whisper, I'm sorry,
I'm so sorry, but you can't control the damn thing. It
has abandoned you. We are both unmade by your
unceasing apologies. The roaches hunger and curse—
fly in zig-zags through the town. They possess. They
build churches. They profess from the altar. They
sleep. They drown. They have families. They devour
their children. They build and tear down empires.
They fail to recycle their plastic water bottles.

He inserts his cock into my ass,
            And there is a sensation.

He says that all of my orifices have pronounced lips,
that it makes me look greedy, like e e e e have never
said no to food or a cock. And yes, yes, this is true. How
does he know me so well?

He inserts his cock into my ass,
        Ahhh resist all sensation. *Ahhhhh will tell you a
story:*

Ahhhhhhhhhhhh have won the king's heart by eating
his only daughter.

She had four breasts, each breast tasted like the
most delicious fruit from the four continents.
Ahhhhhhhhhhhhhhhhhh devoured
them from left to right, the practice of a studied
gourmand. And from left to right, each was more
succulent than the last.

"Father, father, I am older than funereal rites, yet you would
let this sow eat me?"

The princess was a princess of death.
It leaked from her pores. Pools of black liquid formed
wherever she stood.
Whenever she squeezed a pimple a new vector of
disease was born.

Her teeth had rotted from her skull, but what grew
instead was a flower that resembles teeth. She
couldn't eat in front of the guests, and her father, the
king, was tired of making excuses for her.

He inserts his cock into my ass,
    And makes a proclamation!

"Your first daughter was born when a rat crawled out
of the toilet and made love to you in the bath!"
Yes, yes this is true. But 0 never ever talk about her.
How does he know me so well?

He inserts his cock into my ass,
                    and there is a sensation.

My brother had a theory- he could slurp a boy's soul
out through the mouth of his penis.

& my brother is now dead, dead, dead.
() think only of this. () try to think of the cock, my
colon, it's motility, his colon, the heaving in my gills &
legs, but ()
can't.

 "Dsdffffffffffdssssssdfakdfjfjjjjfjsdfksfdlfkjdfs"
"What did you say?"
"Pray for the souls of the lobsters I have consumed."

One by one he inserts his cocks into my ass,
                    And there are sensationsss.

This lover has many cocks. One has a speech
impediment. Another is coated in evidence: tax
documents, photographs, screenshots, transcriptions,
and witness testimony. He will not let me look at this
cock before insertion. But after he is done with me,
[REDACTED] can read traces of his guilt in the paper
cuts left behind on my flesh.
[REDACTED] have to keep numbing cream with me
at all times, because he also has a cock with four
sets of wings that never stop fluttering.
And of course, one cock, has a proboscis that furls
and unfurls, but it is very delicate, and
[REDACTED] have to be careful during our love
making—[REDACTED] must maintain the
architectural integrity of my vessel at all times.

He slid his cock into my asshole,
             And there was an accusation:

He slid his cock into my asshole,
                    And there was a sensation.

Your colon is haunted he says, I can feel ghosts
tapping messages on the head of my penis.

12341234 flail my arms and make a gesture.

He slid his cock into my asshole,
                    And there was a sensation.

He asked me if /// had given birth to any daughters,
and if they were in the house, and where in the house
exactly? And were they behind locked doors? And
where were the keys? And /// told him
that /// hated talking about daughters or the dead, but
if we must, /// said:

/// have given birth to four daughters and all my
daughters are dead. The eldest was thin, sharp,
and mobile, the second soon followed, and she was
mobile, sharp, and thick; and a third was born with
many years in between, she was thick, blunt, and
mobile, the youngest, of course, was thick, blunt, and
immobile.

And the lover, whose cock was still inside me, asked
where were the keys to the bedrooms of the dead
daughters? And /// told him, the doors locked from
the inside. My daughters would lock themselves in
and swallow the key every night. This was to ensure
that they had healthy bowel movements before they
went out into the world.

He slid his cock into my asshole,

& there was weather.

His cock is in my ass and there are no sensations, and even though he is a living thing, I am aware that parts of his body are dead things.

I breathe his scent in deeply and smell the locusts stirring beneath the soil and I know this particular lover will be dead before the day is over.

And my lips are red and full of blood and I feel vitality pumping through my veins, but not his, no not his.

I tell him to stop thrusting and he says, *I haven't finished yet* & I say, well, *I have no use for limp dead cock* and he gets angry, refuses to unwind his body from mine. My anus evaporates along with his sex organs.

As it turns out, both of us will die tonight.

My body transforms into a dishwater and then a metal trashcan lid and then and then and then...

He inserts his cock into my ass,
                    There is a sensation

Sometimes when yiyiyiyiyiy am having sex, yiyiyiyiyiy
grow bored. And this time yiyiyiyiyiyiyiyiyi am bored
w/o my consent, so yiyiyiyiyiyiyiyiyiyiyiyiy remind my
lover to remember their father.

yiyiyiyiyiy can feel all the membranes in his body
stiffen. Any moment now, and he could kill me.
yiyiyiyiyiy tell him yiyiyiyiyiy am a holy being & then he
waits for my instructions.

This is what yiyiyiyiyiy say:
Remember giving birth to your father, raising him?
Remember when he couldn't walk, and his bones
were pudding-soft that took eons to harden into a
phosphorous like material? Remember simmering
his softer materials on the stove?

Remember the stories that your father used to tell
you: about witches that lived in forests that boiled
globular children in giants pots and you knew that
you were never meant to identify with the children,
that he was teaching you a lesson about survival and
hatred and living on the margins of temporality. And
you must have thought, what a good lesson for a
moment like this. Here you were with a stove and a
pot and a child in the shape of your father. You were
cooking your ancestors into their beginnings.

The lover interrupts my instructions and says:

Remember when you sneezed and got flour on his
eyelashes? And then you looked into the mirror and
three of your lashes turned translucent?

Yes, yiyiyiyiyiy remember, yiyiyiyiyiy say.

The lover grabs me by the throat. Extracts the three eyelashes in questions with tweezers and swallows them. yiyiyiyiyiy am offended that he does not properly salt them.

He inserts his cock into my ass,
        And there was a sensation.

My mother was a houseplant.

From her aye learned how to thrive under extreme
conditions (see: the art of lurking in the crevices &
how to move easily between the many planes of life
and death).

There is a thin layer of mold covering my waxy
surfaces. It is nearly invisible but not impossible to
detect. Aye will wait for you to smell me, *There*. That is
me.

Aye will never reproduce, aye am stuck perpetually in
a juvenile state. When my family line hits puberty we
grow 40 feet tall, and our hands become the size of
glass doors. Aye sever my own aerial roots, although
aye have not found a way to cull them from my flesh
completely, aye am exploring new methods of
extermination every day.

He sticks his cocks (all my lovers have more than 3) in
my ass &
            there is a sensation

[m,] am acutely aware of the inside of my mouth, how
my tongue feels pressing against my cheek. That
muscle is pure horse power. [m,] [m,] [m,] am surprised it
doesn't burst through the flesh.

[m,] [m,] [m,] remember my childhood home. [m,] [m,] [m,]
remember [m,] [m,] [m,] had to walk on a path through
the woods to reach it. [m,] [m,] [m,] remember each time
[m,] [m,] [m,] had to walk further and further to find it.
Until one day it wasn't there anymore.

Except every time [m,] [m,] [m,] turned on the news and
there was a murder-suicide, arson, or gas explosion,
my house lurked in the background. [m,] [m,] [m,] could
barely make out the face of my mother, shining and
contorted, pressed against a window pane.

He inserts his cock into my ass,
and all sensations vanish.

△ don't know how to write a love letter.

You murdered me and left me to rot in my own bed.

But all corpses are a part of a psychic network.

△ know in this apartment building alone there are
many murdered women just like me, dead, dead, and
dead. △ have never been good at maintaining close
female friendships, even though △ read Ferrante.

There are three △ have grown extremely closed
to. One is stashed underneath her kitchen sink
in an apartment that is on the very top floor. Her
putrescence swells, leaks, and spreads over us
all. Another woman is hidden behind dry wall.
Another woman curled under the floorboards of her
adolescent daughter's bed.

There is a fourth woman, who is in fact in the next
apartment, folded up into a dirty laundry hamper. She
does not talk though, but when you are dead, you do
not have to. It is so wonderful.

He inserts his coccyx into my ass-O,
                    and there are sensations

eyeeyeeye can barely hold them all in.

His breath is hot rancid garbage on the back of my
neck. Eyeyeyeyeyeye suck it down like a mewling
newborn, Like eyeyeyeyeyeye have never had a drop
of liquid in my parched throat, like the earth was
turning and like eyeyeyeyeyeyeyeeye couldn't feel
death (it's- his – mine) unraveling in my breasts like
eyeyeeyeyeyey use the word breasts and not the
more affable "tits." Like eyeyeyeyeye can hold them in
my hands, like they wouldn't spill out of my fingers,
flooding our bodies, pinning us to the bed, softly
lapping at our holes like hot lava.

He inserts his cock into my ass,
there is a sensation.

Here is my dress. It is sheer and pink and easy to open
and...(symbol) ask, have you ever swallowed your own
seeds? Were you afraid of what you would plant in
your own belly? Did you rub pesticide on your skin like
lotion (symbol) realize this is a mistake to ask, because
no matter what you say (symbol) cannot believe you
for my own survival's sake.

Inside my mouth are cockroaches
And inside their jaws are miniature versions of my ex-lovers.
They are dead and dead and dead and... you curse
me for inviting into the bedroom and our lives and
(symbol) wax eloquently about how the dead are
meant to be held in the mouth to prevent tooth &
spiritual decay.

(symbol) have never had a cavity.

He inserts his cock into my ass
Sometimes when → am having sex ← am filled with revulsion.

And no, no → cannot stop.

Because the word "stop" feels like it exists somewhere
in the bottom of my belly and there is a whole ocean
between it and my larynx.

But this is not one of those times. But still, ← am
remembering one of those times now.

→ try to focus on the sensation.
← close my eyes and clench my jaw.

My tongue, its roots, go numb, my trachea, the left
lung, then right.
"Numb" is the wrong word, → think what ← meant
is that they went "silent." They didn't speak to
me anymore. One by-one each cell in my body
disappears, major organs cease functioning then
vanish until nothing of → ← is left.

He inserts his cock into my ass,
                    and there is a sensation.

👁 think 👁 will keep a record
👁 think 👁 will keep a record
👁 think 👁 will keep a record
👁 think 👁 will keep a record of sensations
👁 think 👁 will keep a record of smells
👁 think 👁 will keep a record of smells associated
with my own body: Lilies, oil of behen nut, sweet flag,
public latrine, rotting fish, grapeseed oil, milk with a
hint of sourness, menstruations of a young girl, the
spit of an old woman, swirling bacteria, cat shit, my
shit, wine, burnt offerings, dogs dying in the heat...

👁 can smell me no matter where 👁 go. A cock
froths up the stenches, changes the way the notes
intermingle and reveals...

::

I wander the earth, hungry for semen

⟨⟨⟨
⟩⟩⟩

The author wishes to acknowledge the insight and generosity of Rachel Zavecz, Jace Brittain, Kellie Wells, Michael Martone, Jessica Kidd, Amy Dayton, TSWT, Heidi Staples, and the bi-uncles.

Cat Ingrid Leeches wrote what preceded.

WL drew what was drawn.

Dreams, myths, fragments, confessionals, and chapters from this book appeared as forms in *Passages North*, *fugue*, *The Offing*, *Taurpaulin Sky*, *Nat. Brut*, *the Adroit Journal*, *Hayden's Ferry Review*, and other journals.

Garden Door Press published a book called *The Connoisseur*.

Jace Brittain and Rachel Zavecz edited this volume as Carrion Bloom Books.